S0-BFH-018

THE
SINGING
FLUTE

GURDON S. WORCESTER

Illustrated by Irene Burns

HALSEY PUBLISHING COMPANY, INC.

THE SINGING FLUTE

© 1963 by Gurdon S. Worcester

All rights reserved.

No part of this publication may be reproduced, stored in a retrieval system, or transmitted in any form or by any means without the prior written permission of Halsey Publishing Company, Inc., 2 Park Avenue, New York, N.Y. 10016.

Library of Congress Catalog Card Number 73-81345

ISBN 0-913634-15-8

Foreword

On beginning to read *The Singing Flute*, I felt drawn to it because, at first glance, it appears to be laid in a setting close to my heart — Cape Ann, the rocky, ocean-swept promontory in northern Massachusetts where I have spent more than forty summers. The little girl protagonist, Hilli, is Finnish; one of the pure blond, sun-bronzed, strong, courageous people who, since they came over late in the last century to work the quarries, have been among Cape Ann's finest, certainly its handsomest, inhabitants. The smell of bayberry and sweet fern, of salt and sunshine, the sound and sight of the sea, the quarry pools like cups set in the rosy granite, the paper-white birches, the mysterious cellars on Dogtown Common: these things that I love and know are all in *The Singing Flute*.

But as I got farther into the story, and read it again, it was borne in upon me that the setting of the story is not really Cape Ann at all; or rather it is Cape Ann and at the same time another place familiar to all who know Andersen, know the Arabian Nights, know Grimm and Perrault and Beatrix Potter and Isak Dinesen. Fairyland is only one of its names. For centuries it has been the setting for tales as disparate as the Mowgli stories and *At the Back of the North Wind*, tales whose names are music to our memories: *Snow white and Rose Red* and *The City of Bronze*. It is a land where pure imagination reigns.

What sort of images does imagination ordain there? One writer on fairy stories said recently: "Their moral universe is simple, though sometimes with subtle undertones: the struggle of good against evil, with the weaker protagonist on the side of good and always winning." I would go farther and point out that the moral universe of fairy tales can be highly complex. One realizes, when a fairy tale returns to haunt one's memory, that it is not so much a story about some protagonist goose-girl or third son, as it is a mirror held up to a vast being of whom the story's characters are merely the members and whose name is legion.

The fairy tale is everyone, and its secret is the elusive common plight. When I read a fairy story, the sleeping princess is me, and so is the prince to whom she cries: "I have been waiting for you so long!" The hideous Beast, too, is me, as well as she who by pronouncing the words "I will, dear Beast," turns him into someone longed for and delightful. It is this depth which makes the good and the enduring story—for children are instinctively as bored by the shallow as their elders consciously are.

The Singing Flute is a true work of the imagination. For example, what is one to make of the mysterious and significant lameness that links Uncle Lauri and the child Hilli, both sensitive and life-loving, as against the queerly legendary harshness of the father, Torni? Who, indeed, *is* Lauri — so like Orpheus, like Pan? What is the tune Lauri plays on his flute, first to Torni's young wife whose life is crushed out through her husband's harshness; then, in almost a reliving of the scenes, to her little daughter? What is the secret of the flute as it lies just below the surface of the dark quarry pool? And who is the strange black dog who is part killer, part savior? I can only ask the questions. I can't answer them. That is what fairy stories are for: to tell the untellable.

In a day when the Sorcerer's Apprentice would appear to be in charge of the production of children's books, it is good to come upon a tale like *The Singing Flute*, which is in so many ways what a child's story ought to be: familiar without being banal, imaginative yet faithful to daily life, exciting and magical to a child, and for its parent, a joy and a reward.

Nancy Hale

The
Singing
Flute

Hilli was walking quietly along the forbidden road.
Perhaps, on this first day of summer, if she went
softly she might hear her Uncle Lauri playing his flute.
Perhaps she could get a glimpse through the birch
trees of his little house. She might even see him. He
never spoke and you never heard him coming — that
was what made it so exciting. He was simply there,
as if he had been waiting, standing under the trees
and looking at her with a smile that made her ache
with happiness and a strange, shy longing. The trouble
between her father and her uncle had started long
ago, before she was born, but she knew about it, just
as she understood that she must never take the path
that led through the valley.

1

Hilli was only eleven, but she was moved by mysterious forces. How could she help it? Her middle name was Mielikki, the Spirit of the Woodland in the ancient Finnish legend of the Kalevala, and so, as Queen of the Forest, she was able to see and hear things that other people never could.

Now she heard the sound that always made her feel weak with delight and powerless to turn back — the little tune she knew Lauri had made for her. It had in it the singing of the wind in the pines, the chuckling of squirrels and of the brook that tumbled down under the leaves, the way her heart did now. She dropped her schoolbooks and sat down, leaning against a great boulder to listen.

She opened her eyes when the music stopped and knew it was time to go home. But someone was standing in the shadow of the trees. Their eyes met, and the lights in Lauri's started something dancing inside her that grew and grew until they were laughing together as if there were nothing else in all the world.

And yet there was something more, something she wanted terribly to tell him but couldn't find the words. She swallowed, looking away, and when she turned back, Lauri was gone.

She was late for supper, and now, starting on the long climb home, she felt the tiredness of her limping foot. Two years before, Hilli had been sick and had had to learn to walk all over again. Although she was still behind in geography at school, she knew

every trail and path, every forgotten wagon track, from Dogtown Common to Folly Cove.

As the shadows lengthened, she imagined the plunging horses that once dragged stoneboats down this very road to the barges waiting in the harbor. Years ago, even before her father could remember, stonecutters had come from Finland to Massachusetts to work in the quarries. This lonely land, with its ledges and moors, its woods of oak and birch and wind-twisted pines, reminded them of their own country. Here they took up their ancient industry, for Cape Ann was a huge cap of granite that lay under the innocent woods and fields and ran out to the headlands of the shore where green seas thundered. Their quarrying by drill and dynamite made the great pits

5

which, abandoned, filled slowly with crystal water and became for them the lakes of home.

These men of stone were giants who lived a stern life founded on rock but lightened with a godlike gift of laughter. They were honest and generous; yet if you threatened their freedom or their land you found them as hard as the granite they quarried. Nothing is warmer than Finnish friendship and nothing colder than a black feud.

The trouble between Hilli's father and his brother had happened long ago, but there were those who still remembered. Things are borne on the wind in Little Finland. Although people mind their own business, there is little they don't know about their neighbors. On wet or snowy days it was a long way home from school, and sometimes the old lady who lived in the last house from the village would tap on her window and beckon Hilli inside. In the spotless blue and white kitchen that smelled of fresh bread and strong coffee, Hilli would sit and drink milk and listen to the saga of days she had only imagined.

Hilli's grandfather had bought his independence in the new world by toil that ended only when the stone-dust sickness killed him. His oldest son Torni — the

Finnish name for tower — was tall, strong, and sensible. Watching his father die, he became a man overnight in his fierce struggle to save the quarrying business, to hold the land.

He was steady and slow to anger, but he grew used to giving orders, and his will was granite. No one could say that Torni was unjust, or did less than two men's work, but since the day of his father's death, no one had ever heard him laugh.

In his world, where work was everything, his brother was an exasperation. Lauri, whose nickname was Lokki — the sea gull — was five years younger, quick and slender, with dark eyes that read secrets in the clouds and the winds and laughed at the dusty toil of quarry slaves. He helped now and then with ideas, tossed out so carelessly that it was always a surprise when they worked, leaving Torni baffled and silent. But mostly he listened to the birds and practiced the flute.

Watching the old woman's wrinkled face and bright black eyes, Hilli lived every moment of that August afternoon. Torni was behind on his contract with the monument company, and the granite shaft, with one end on the truck, had come to a grinding halt. Lauri, his hands in his pockets, stood aloof, whistling — watching. Perhaps it was the carefree accompaniment to his sweating labor that stung Torni — that and the knowledge that at any moment he might hear of a better way. He stopped, mopping his face, and saw

8

the smile dancing in Lauri's eyes. He snatched up a crowbar and thrust it into his brother's hands. "But look," Lauri said.

"But work!" Torni roared, and they went on, with Lauri's tune softer and his brother taking bite after bite with his great bar. The shaft inched up, then jammed again. Lauri's whistling was like a stinging gadfly. Torni turned on the torment, and then it happened. There was a crunching roar as the stone shot back and off the truck, pinning Lauri's leg beneath it.

The next instant Torni was on the ground, his feet braced, his giant shoulders lifting. The shaft rolled heavily over, revealing the crushed, bleeding leg. For one moment Torni met his brother's eyes before they closed in a faint.

The leg was saved, but it was a long time before Lauri could walk again, and always with a limp. Now he kept the books for his brother in their tiny office, drew designs for monuments, and played the flute through the summer evenings. Although Torni treated him with dogged kindness, things were different, and Lauri was brooding and restless.

Then, astonishingly, Torni married. Hilja, who had recently come from Finland, was a shy, lovely girl with pale gold hair and eyes like the sea over sand. She loved Torni but she was desperately homesick and lost in the remote quarry land. Alone in the house, she would stop her work to listen to Lauri's flute, and sometimes in the afternoon she would walk over to

the little office with a piece of sweet Finnish bread and glass of milk. Torni saw how her face lighted whenever Lauri played, or came by, and he grew even more silent and worked more fiercely than ever.

One afternoon, when he came home from the black-smith's with newly sharpened drills, Hilja was nowhere to be seen. From far off he heard the faint notes of a flute and followed the sound.

She was with Lauri, by the little pit. Torni saw her listening, spellbound, and a strange fear took hold of him. What had brought this look into her face? He stood unseen, watching.

10

The music was *Finlandia*, as only an exile, lost and far from home, might hear it. It sang of a white country, silent under the frosty starlight; of dark forests, of crystal lakes beneath the blue of a summer sky. It sang with longing and with love.

As the last notes died away, Torni was shaken. All that mattered was Hilja's look, the magic by which the flute enchanted her. He stepped out on the ledge.

"This is how you keep my house," he said. Then, with a flash, to Lauri: "And my accounts."

"But the house is kept," Hilja pleaded, "and there's no more to do."

Lauri said: "The accounts are settled, and no need to waste a day like this."

Something flamed in Torni. "There's one account to settle——"

He felt his brother's new courage as Lauri rose to his feet. "Poor Torni," he said. "You understand only hardness. But you'll be betrayed by things you cannot break."

"Like you?"

"Like music that you cannot hear," Lauri said. "Like laughter that you cannot bear, and the secrets of the wind and water——"

"You are the music and laughter that betray me," Torni cried, "and you will find the hardness of life when I let you go."

Lauri left that night. On their father's old blue map a line was drawn dividing the land. For his share he took only the worthless part where the brook ran through the valley. Now Torni and Hilja were alone together, but he saw in her eyes that a magic had gone from the world.

After she died in childbirth, he was a different man. He worked alone, now, cutting building stone near his house, and Hilli grew up to the sound of hammer and drill. Though their land adjoined, the two brothers lived in bitter and silent loneliness.

When the old woman finished speaking, Hilli sat looking at her quietly. At last she thanked her and said goodbye. As she walked away, she felt different and older. For now she knew, and perhaps some day, somehow. . . .

That winter's day seemed very far off on this warm June evening. The road had climbed to a windswept hill, and there in the sunset light was the little stone house with her father standing by the door. He was a huge man with reddish-gold hair and massive shoulders. His eyes, bluer than the sea, saw more than Hilli dared to think.

"You take a long time coming home," he said, and she felt a stab. "And a long way round," he added.

She kissed him before he could say more, and hurried with supper because she'd done something secret and wrong. But her guilty feelings didn't last, for after all, how could she tell him things she didn't understand herself, like the magic of Lauri's playing? Besides, he wouldn't be cross for long. He wasn't really rough and hard, as others found him. It was only that her mother's death had left him helpless, baffled at finding that there were things the strongest hands could never hold. And with Hilli he was always gentle.

Looking at him across the supper table, she remembered the time after she had come back from the hospital, when she had shown him how well she could walk. Each day he took her hand and went beside her with short, shuffling steps. As her own steps lengthened, his smile grew. And then one day when she was strong enough to venture out alone, she went all the way to the little quarry above the valley. On that hot afternoon, the water lay so cool and green that a wonderful plan came to her and she hurried back to tell her father.

He was waiting at the house, and she almost ran into his arms. He smiled, picking her up. "I went such a long way," she told him, "and I thought that if I could only learn to swim this summer, in the little. . . ."

"No."

Hilli had never heard that voice before, and then she remembered that he had almost drowned in one of the quarries when he was a boy. He'd had no time

from work to learn to swim with the others. She tried again. "But the doctor said. . . ."

"No, never."

Her real help came from the woods, whose call she was frantic to answer after months in bed. How could a Queen of the Forest lie ill when all her world was waiting? From the first day, the remembered trails filled her with excitement. Hilli forgot her dragging foot, for she could still find the hidden pool where trout rings were reflected in golden bands that

mingled and swam upward on the black cliff. She could still see the lady's slippers gleaming in the dark ravine and hear the bee tree humming in the burnt-over meadow. Now at last, with everything as it should be, she could lay her cheek against the warm earth, close her eyes, and smell the bayberry and sweet fern that made her nose prickle.

Perhaps because he loved seeing her grow stronger, Torni allowed her to go as she pleased and never asked her where. And so, because he understood, she told him all her adventures — or almost all. For there were times in her realm of deep woods and sunlit pools when she found the very spirit of laughter. Lauri shared her world of clouds and starlight; he, too, was lame, but he moved with the silence and secrecy of foxes and deer and birds of the air.

Now, after supper, sitting across the hearth from her father, Hilli smiled, thinking of school being over, of all the wonders that waited for her in the long summer.

Her father's voice was quiet. "What makes you so happy?"

19

She couldn't tell him it was because she loved him so. But maybe about the brook. . . . She slipped out of her chair to put her arms around his neck and whisper in his ear: "I'm going exploring tomorrow, to find out where the brook goes near Dogtown——"

He interrupted her. "I wouldn't go that far, Hilli. There may be shooting."

She lifted her head to stare. "But hunters don't come until fall."

"These are men from the town," he told her. "They're hunting a dog that's gone wild."

"But why do they have to——"

Torni told her how the old stonemason had lived alone in a cabin near the moors; how friends, looking for him, had found his great black beast, half-starved and savage, guarding the door. They had had to beat the dog off with clubs to bring his dead master down. He had followed all the way, but when the village dogs set on him he had left two for dead and gone back to range the moors for rabbits and whatever food he could find. Woodcutters returning at dusk told of being haunted by an enormous shadow with eyes like coals. The town had become aroused, and now men were going out to shoot him.

Hilli was pushing slowly away. "But what if he's only lost and hungry? What if——"

"He's a killer." The words were final. "I'll tell you when you can go to Dogtown."

She slid off his knee and stood by his chair unhappily. Suddenly all her hopes of the summer seemed darkened. She waited for him to speak again, and when he didn't she went slowly upstairs.

In bed, Hilli closed her eyes very tightly, then fell into a sleep that was troubled with dreams of frantic searching for a dog through a black forest filled with hunters. She woke to find her room silver with moonlight and knew why she couldn't sleep. Outside, on this brightest, whitest summer night, all her voices were calling.

She put on her wrapper and went noiselessly down the narrow stairs. Below, she listened for a moment to be sure her father was asleep before she slipped out. Crystal stars glittered in the enormous sky and the dew made jewels that washed her bare feet with cold fire. The path through the woods was a tunnel with the moon shut out, but she could tell every turning, every root and hollow.

And then, in one instant, the woods ended and Hilli was standing by the vast majesty and stillness of Black Pool. Her path lay along a dark cliff over which the grout pile loomed — a mountain of granite blocks hewn from the depths of the earth and piled by giants long ago. Picking her way over the great

slabs, she climbed to the stone at the very top. It's curved back that formed her throne was still warm from the sun.

As the orchestra tuned up, Hilli listened to the voices that made up her symphony: the scrapings of the crickets, the fluting notes of the night birds, the tiny fifings of the bats that turned so swiftly against the moon; the deep-plucked strings of the bullfrogs, and, far away, the bugling of hounds across the valley.

Then, in a moment of stillness, it came — the sound of Lauri's flute. It started with the song of the thrush, choiring down the night. It fell like a net that caught the silver of the stars and spread shimmering over the woodland. It must be a brother to the wind, she thought, for it whispered through the grasses, spilled like moonlight over the still water, and died in the silence and dreaming of the valley. It flooded her with a happiness that was almost pain, but when it ended she felt restless and strange. At last she rose and went quietly down the shadowy paths that led to home and bed.

Hilli woke in the morning to find the sun high, her father gone, and her mind made up. She dusted and tidied the house more carefully than usual, for this was the first time she had ever really disobeyed him. She cut as much meat as she dared and wrapped it with her sandwiches, hurrying, for it was almost noon.

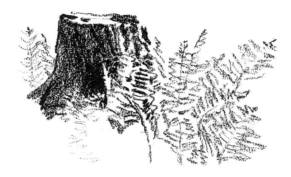

Reaching the woods, she went softly along the leafy path, playing her old game of seeing how far she could steal into the squirrels' country before they caught her. But then a stick cracked under foot and the game was over.

"Cheat, cheat!" The bluejays' alarm filled the woods. Hilli saw the flashes of blue and black as they shrieked her crime from the treetops. She felt for the bread crumbs in her pocket, and the birds, swooping to the path, forgot her. Then, like little gray policemen answering a whistle, the squirrels came rushing from branch to branch until they hunched overhead, bursting with rage.

"You're just mad because I fooled you." She tossed out a handful of dried peas and instantly the scolding stopped. The squirrels dropped down to munch and watch her with black button-eyes. When they could eat no more they buried the rest and then began their flying circus, whipping after each other and flashing up and down and round and round the trunk of the great beech tree.

She ought to go, but she stood looking back. If she could only keep this moment, hide it away as they hid the peas, then some dark winter's day she might remember the dappling sunlight on the brown path and the old gray beech tree with its laughing wreath of squirrels.

As Hilli started on, they fled up again until they vanished high above her and she heard only the clash of leaves far ahead. She reached the brook and wondered once more where it went, but she thought of the dog and the hunters and hurried on. Finally the woods ended and she came out on the green-brown stretch of Dogtown Common. She searched for a long time among the black junipers that stood like sentries and around stones that marked the cellars of ancient houses. At last she sat down on a lichened boulder and remembered that she was hungry.

She was unwrapping her sandwiches when she felt a dark shadow. She looked up and her heart almost stopped. At first glance, the black monster was terrifying, with his huge head, his bloodshot eyes, and the broom-grass in his rough coat. Then she saw his thin ribs and sides caved in from hunger. Hilli took out a piece of meat and held it toward him cautiously. He moved a step forward, took it gently from her fingers and, in a gulp, it was gone. She fed him another, then another, and one by one all her sandwiches, watching the same gentleness, the sudden wolfing. At last she showed him her empty hands. "That's all," she said, and he dipped his head in an awkward little gambol, ending in a yelp.

She got up, laughing, ready to coax him back, but as she started toward the path she saw him whirl and turned to see three figures rise menacing against the sky. The dog crouched, growling, a great ruff rising around his neck. Hilli sank her fingers in it and tried to pull him away, but he shook her off. As the men spread out, his head dropped and he sprang from side to side to face then, snarling.

The men waved her away and their guns came up. She looked back at the dog. As she saw his thinness, his trembling frame, and remembered his foolish

gambol, something stronger than fear took hold of her. Standing beside him with one arm around his neck, she saw the guns go slowly down and the men draw together, talking. At last they backed away as silently as they had come.

The huge dog walked ahead of Hilli along the path, stopping from time to time to look back into her face; then he moved on with his tail waving victoriously. At the brook he splashed in and lapped the icy water. Suddenly he lifted his head to listen, an ear cocked sideways and his brow wrinkled. For one moment Hilli thought of the hunters, but his tail still waved gently. Then she heard the bluejays and laughed. Their piping notes over the squirrels' chirring made a little fife-and-drum corps to lead her and the dog on in triumphal procession. Down they went,

and down, with the music always just ahead. Where was the stream taking them? What if they were lost in the darkening woods? She listened. The music sounded nearer and her heart beat faster, for it was changing to something familiar. It was her own tune that laughed and turned on itself, but now it was ending. Hilli pushed through a thick screen of alders, and then she knew.

The mossy clearing stretched green and gold, and there among the birches by his door stood Lauri. The flute glittered in his long fingers and he was smiling, his head back. The pointed chin, the forehead rising in two peaks to hair like leaves — where

31

had she seen a statue like this, in what picture, of what old garden? She saw the dog walk slowly forward to stand at his feet with lowered head; she saw Lauri drop to one knee and put his arm around him.

Watching them together, Hilli thought that if she slipped away now they would never notice. Besides, it was late, and time to go.

So this was where the brook had led, and how the tune had ended. She ought to be happy, but she was suddenly terribly tired, and as she turned away all the green and gold blurred in a mist of tears. Were they for these two outcasts who had found each other, or for someone who was lost and lonely, walking up the darkening road to home?

When she reached the house, her father had finished his supper and was standing silently at the window in the other room. While she got her own and washed the dishes, Hilli waited, half fearfully, for him to speak. She wanted terribly to tell him about the day's adventure, but. . . .

Then, through the open window, she heard it, clear and silvery as the evening star. Lauri's music poured over her heart like an end of loneliness. She stole a glance at her father. If he could only hear!

32

But in one stride he had crossed the room and closed the window, and something was shut between them. He stood, huge against the last light, and spoke without turning. "Have you ever seen your Uncle Lauri?"

"Yes," Hilli said. "I've seen him."

"Do you ever speak with him?"

"No, never." She drew a breath. "I only listen."

After a moment, Torni asked, "What does he tell you?"

She looked out toward the lost music. "His playing told me." She found it hard to speak, but she went on: "It told about a place where there was laughter and——"

Her father's voice was different. "Where?"

"Just somewhere. I never found out." Hilli stopped, helpless. Then, because she felt as if something were breaking inside her, she turned quickly away.

Her father never spoke about her finding the dog; yet, as the summer went on, Hilli was sure he knew. And then, all at once, the days were growing shorter, more golden and precious. School began, but there was still time to walk in her world.

Sometimes, in the autumn, hunters came through the wild quarry land, though her father warned them off. One October afternoon, Torni was working late

and she was alone. Soon windows would be shut against the cold. Before the woods and music were lost to her, she could take one last walk, not by the road, but only to the little pit above the valley.

Hilli was approaching it when she heard the shot and, a moment later, saw the wounded duck. It came in on a long, wavering curve, hitting the water with a great splash. Then, on her left, she heard a deep bark. The black dog was rushing with long bounds through the bracken and, without slowing his pace, he plunged out and down. He came up shaking his head and swam straight to retrieve the dying bird, then made for the shallow end.

He was halfway up the bank of stone chips when Hilli caught sight of Lauri standing by the twisted pine at the edge. Turning to follow his eyes, she saw

34

her father striding toward them. As Torni advanced, his brother waited, motionless, the dead bird at his feet. Her father came on and she heard the rumble begin deep in the dog's throat, but Lauri's fingers twisted in the ruff that had risen around the giant head.

Hilli had never heard her father's voice so terrible. "That dog is a killer. If he comes on my land once more, I'll shoot him."

As if he hadn't heard, Lauri turned to Hilli, and she felt the old joy sweep over her, for he smiled, lifting his flute. It was the little fife-and-drum tune that had led her down the brook, and she laughed, remembering. Then she looked quickly at her father, and froze. He was staring from her to his brother as if he were seeing some ghost of long ago.

Lauri laid his flute on the ledge and bent down. He put one hand on the massive black shoulders and the dog's eyes held his. With his other hand sweeping along the boundary of woods, he gave a low command. The dog moved slowly off among the trees.

The next instant, Hilli saw her father take two quick steps, snatch up the flute and throw it far out. It turned, flashing in the sunset light, and she heard the sound — a sobbing music made on the wind, a last mournful cry that was choked in the black water.

The silence was like thunder. Lauri stood deathly still, but his eyes held lightnings of another world. Before them, her father's wavered and fell. He took her hand, and, without a word, turned back toward home.

That winter was longer and darker than ever before. Even in their wordless language there were silences. Hilli went to school and came back, but there was nothing to tell her father. Something was frozen in her, just as all her secret paths were blocked with snow. She got their supper and did the dishes and her homework as if everything were still the same, but each knew it wasn't. Sometimes, sitting by the fire, she would see a spark like a falling star and remember the flute; then she would put down her book to listen. She felt a coldness the fire could never warm, and heard high overhead in the chimney the cry of the avenging winds.

As the winter wore away, Hilli was filled with a queer restlessness. One warm afternoon at the end of March she found that down by the spring the willow was turning, but in the shade of the grout pile there were still the tailings of winter. That night she knelt by her open window looking out over the valley and felt something breathing in the woods. A longing took hold of her that kept her on her knees until she shivered and made it hard for her to get to sleep.

Next morning was the start of vacation, and Hilli could scarcely wait to set out. Walking toward the little quarry, she saw that the snow was gone except for patches of white in the hollows; yet the world seemed locked in the grip of winter. Under a torn gray sky, the woods were black and silent. Where were

the stirrings she had felt the night before? Where
were her voices, the whispering promise of spring?
A terrible fear seized her. What if summer never came?

When Hilli reached the little pit, pale panes of ice
were still floating. She looked toward the low cliff
under which the flute had vanished in the black water
and stood listening to the silence of the valley; then
she walked slowly around the edge of the deep pool,
stopped at the cliff side and looked over.

She saw it first as a mysterious light that trembled from below, and held her breath. There, on a ledge not very far down, something gleamed with a white fire that made her shiver with excitement. Moving cautiously, she lowered herself to the narrow step at the water's edge. Yes, there was Lauri's flute, a silver wand with its magic drowned — the laughter and singing of summertime lost below the wind. It was almost within reach.

She fumbled, pushing up her sleeve. With one hand she held a tiny birch that was growing out of a seam in the cliff, leaned down and felt the stinging water on her bare arm. As she reached farther, the living, dancing light filled her eyes.

Hilli gave a cry as the sapling's root pulled out and she plunged down. With her eyes closed tight against the freezing blackness, her hand grasped something slender and smooth. Her lungs were bursting, but her head came above the surface and she drew one gulping breath. She tried to call again but couldn't. Her skirt clung, her leg was numb and useless, but she held desperately to the flute.

In that instant, she heard a roaring bark and saw the black form hurtling out and down. The last thing she knew before she sank was his huge head coming straight for her. Hilli felt the tug of her coat, the massive lift, the air again, the steady strength of his driving body. Then enormous hands were lifting her and her father strode up the crunching slope. Her weight was nothing, but she heard him breathe as if he were carrying the whole world.

At the top, Torni put her down, took off his coat and wrapped her in it. She saw the rifle as he bent to pick it up. He broke it across his knee like a toy and hurled the pieces into the pit. He lifted her again and started walking, not back toward home, but onward and down, while the great dog moved ahead.

Now, in her father's arms, still holding the flute, Hilli saw a miracle. For here in the valley, green things were putting out and high overhead in the trees the winds were hushed to a murmer. A heavenly warmth was stealing over her, a happiness like music . . . like laughter. . . .

And there by his door stood Lauri, as if he had been waiting always. He was smiling, and the light in his eyes was like the warmth she had found, like the summer sun. Her father set her down. She saw his arms lift in a gesture that was huge and helpless; then, as he stumbled forward, they went around his brother.

At last Torni stepped back and looked at Lauri. And, for the first time, Hilli heard her father's laughter. It was like an unbound torrent in spring. It rose from the rocks and spread through the woodland around them. It filled the whole world, and her own heart to bursting.

Lauri picked her up, and, with one arm around his brother, he brought them into his little house.